Rattlesnake Plantain

HEIDI GRECO

Rattlesnake Plantain

ANVIL PRESS | VANCOUVER

Rattlesnake Plantain
Copyright © 2002 by Heidi Greco

Anvil Press
6 West 17th Avenue
Vancouver, B.C. V5Y IZ4   CANADA

The publisher gratefully acknowledges the financial assistance of the B.C. Arts Council, the Canada Council for the Arts, and the Book Publishing Industry Development Program (BPIDP) for their support of our publishing program.

NATIONAL LIBRARY OF CANADA CATALOGUING IN PUBLICATION DATA

Greco, Heidi.
    Rattlesnake plantain

Poems.
ISBN I-895636-43-4

    I. Title
PS8563.R41452R37 2002   C811'.6   C2002-910941-8
PR9199.4.G73R37 2002

Printed and bound in Canada
Cover design: Rayola Graphic Design
Author photo: George Omorean
Represented in Canada by the Literary Press Group
Distributed by the University of Toronto Press

BRITISH
COLUMBIA
ARTS COUNCIL
Supported by the Province of British Columbia

The Canada Council | Le Conseil des Arts
for the Arts | du Canada

For Carole
who thought she ran out of time

Acknowledgements

Some of these poems, or versions of these poems, have appeared in the following publications:
Contemporary Verse 2, ink, Other Voices, Quarter Moon Quarterly, Room of One's Own, sub-TERRAIN, Words

ANTHOLOGIES:
Chickweed (Sage Hill Chapbooks, 1999), *Friendly Erotica: A Question of Boundaries* (Martin Park Communications, 1996), *Study in Grey: Women Writing about Depression* (Rowan Books, 1999)

AND AT THE FOLLOWING WEBSITES:
www.wtc.ab.ca/tedyck/RedNeck.htm
www3.telus.net/greenboathouse/poetrypage.htm
www.lights.com/sagehill/alumni/index.html

The phrase, 'the twelve colours of darkness' is from a piece entitled "Poem" by David Malouf.

All flower definitions in the section "Time of the Angel" are from *Wildflowers Across the Prairies* by F.R. Vance, J.R. Jowsey, J.S. McLean and Francis Switzer. Published by Greystone Books (Douglas & McIntyre Publishing Group), Vancouver/Toronto, 1993.

With gratitude to the B.C. Arts Council for assistance.

Table of Contents

Time of the Angel

Raceme: *A flower cluster with each flower borne on a short stalk arising at different points on a common stem.*

from *Wildflowers Across the Prairies*
F.R.Vance and J.R.Jowsey

Notes from Underground

Cattail *(Typha latifolia): The pale green upper spike carries the male flowers and disappears, usually due to being broken off. . . . Growth habit is perennial from thick creeping roots.*

I want to tip the gravestones
see what's written in the soil
by those fingers working underground
shaping sturdy words

cold truths in the darkness
must be easier to find
all that softened quiet time
hidden safe away

clearer than my standing here
this side all this light
up here in the glare of day
such easy distractions

Where Blackberries are Red

Wild Red Raspberry *(Rubus idaeus): Fruit is a berry of many fleshy drupelets.... It is bright red when ripe.... Although not considered to have an economic value, it has been a valuable addition...to the diets of many people ever since man came to the plains of North America.*

I come from a cold place
snowy and frozen too hard all the winter
hot and unfriendly as snakeballs all summer

November's browned grasses
rub my ankles raw
aggravate the itch of woolen leggings

I walk my way through stony fields
weave circles through the weeds
avoiding heading back to
the house I go to sleep in
that room too full of corners
where only my clothes seem to live

purple-headed thistles
tear my knees annoy my shins
rounded burrs ride the tail of my shoelace

I build forts shrines nests of flowers
place wild crowns in hollow trees

all I want is someplace with
blackberries on the vines
red but so much sweeter
than are these upon my tongue

Before the Time of the Angel

Baby's Breath *(Gypsphila paniculata): Flowers are white to pale pink...borne on numerous panicled cymes to give the whole plant the appearance of a puff of mist.*

when he told her
she had pre-Raphaelite hair
she had some subtle intuition
even though she didn't know
the meaning of the phrase

she understood his words to mean
before the time of the angel
and wondered if that was something like
how Mary the Virgin had looked
before that angel filled her
with terror and light

First Day in Somalia, 1992

Skeletonweed (*Lygodesmia juncea*): *The plant...appears as a "jungle" of bare, rigid, tough stems topped by a few flower heads. The stems release a milky juice when broken.*

we are intruders
stark and out of place
standing in gritty wind
visitors to an alien part of the planet

our loosely-fitted cotton clothes
bear designer tags
the bagginess a mockery
their fashion statement lost
on the skeletons
who huddle in this camp

we wear cameras
and sunglasses
tote accessory bags
grumble as we lug around
more wealth on our shoulders
than these people will know within their lifetimes

the graininess that rides the air
strains at our relationships
all of us complain of the heat
about the parch at the back of our throats

a woman
very beautiful
despite the angled points
quizzical geometries of bones pronging out
such unlikely joinings in her body
turns to face against the wind
reveals a narrow boy

like some heron dressed in rags
he is barely there
one leg bent up sharply at the knee

slender as a shadow
he leans himself against her
stretches his hand into her dress
searches the folds of cloth
pulls out the sagging flap of her breast
holds its withered tip between his lips

lowering our cameras
we glance at one another
raise an eyebrow
shift our feet
no need to say a word

silently we damn the sight
this vision of perversion
he is standing tall enough

beside his mother's chest
to encircle her in his arms
nearly a man

later
we discover
that the man/child was eleven
he is dead now
that her baby
has been taken

LOST IN ZAIRE: QUESTIONS FROM A SON WHO WATCHES TOO MUCH NEWS

Common Mullein *(Verbascum thapsus): Leaves are alternate, medium to dark green, and velvety due to many branched hairs. . . . Habitat is roadsides, garden edges, field margins, or otherwise disturbed land.*

you're worried
I know you are
about those kids lost by the side of the road
ones the bands of people
moved too fast for

worried
they were the kind of kids
who liked to look at things
maybe had to pee
wanted to play for a minute or so
with a pile of broken rocks balanced in the dust
throw a stick a dog might want to fetch

worried
if we'd been walking
carrying all we owned on our heads
on our backs
after too many nights of bugs and thieves
not enough to eat or drink

would we have maybe gone
forgotten you by the road someplace too

      come down into the kitchen
      drink some milky tea
      hold my hand
      sit in my lap
      please
      while you still fit here

STUDY IN GREY

__Wild Licorice__ (Glycyrrhiza lepidota): Fruit is an oblong bur-like pod...densely covered with hooked prickles. The dry stems and pods often persist until the next season.

depression wears an old coat
gravy-stained and frayed at the cuffs
pockets long since rotted through
empty holes to hang your hands in
nothing to put in there anyway

it is a grey thing   thick
as yesterday's porridge gone cold
handle of the spoon poking out to one side
bowl stuck to the table
in a ring of sugary milk

notice how sad the old face on the moon is
mouth hanging open   an anguish of oh
small wonder dogs   night coyotes howl reply
madwomen   wolves lie beneath it

baring their bellies unto its cold light
wishing for some scratch of comfort
soothing bath from a softened cloth
grey from too many washings

EXFOLIATION

Leafy Spurge *(Euphorbia esula): Flowers are greenish-yellow, without petals and sepals...capsules burst open with some force when ripe.*

there is no point in old regrets
windows shattered from within
bits of broken glass outside the hen house

wild mosaics scattered there stiffen in the grass
yellow and golden leaves observe
like icons from the trees

breathing jagged through his mouth
the man wipes off his blade
still enjoys the sound of turning knives

CUTTING LINE ACROSS THE NIGHT

Rattlesnake Plantain *(Goodyera repens): Leaves are dark green, obovate. . .very lined and mottled, like the back of a rattlesnake.*

midnight   we are edging the canoe
to the other side of the world
or is it only the other side of the lake
hard to be sure of anything beneath this moonlit sky

we cut a clean bisection
through pointed diamond peaks
like some sideways Rorschach test
patterned steeples rise

clouds and mountains form a string
careless as an unhooked bra
lying there across the lake
in the creamy light

quiet paddles dip and pull
through the sheet of water
lying there so still it wears reflection of a moon
rounded as the one that rides above us

who can say which one is true
if gravity still rules
whether it is a law
we should continue to believe

Waiting for Mortality: Lined Up at the Ferry

Hooded Lady's-Tresses *(Spiranthes romanzoffiana): Flowers are sweet scented...each on a short stalk in three spirals on a spike.... The hood is formed of three sepals and two lateral petals, and in profile looks like the brim of a sunbonnet.... Growth habit is perennial and erect, on rather stout stems.*

three crows in the parking lot
look like fat old ladies
walk as if they wear cheap shoes
that tightly pinch their toes

splayed feet carry too much weight
years of disappointment
bones and corns poke hard inside
leather gone too soft

sagged like tired elastic
worn-out girdles stretched beyond
memories of thinner waists or young men lean and handsome
lined up tall to kiss them all in springtime

*Springbeauty (Claytonia lanceolata): Flowers are white,
occasionally with pink lines or shading on the five petals, star-
shaped. . . . Flowering occurs in May. . . . It is rare but still found
in some places.*

portrait of my mother
nineteen and beautiful
she holds a petalled flower
close beside her cheek
listening
a phone call from the past

La Mariposa Blanca (White Butterfly)

Saskatoon *(Amelanchier alnifolia): Flowers are white...with five rounded petals and five sepals. They are borne in multiple clusters at the ends of branches...*

floppy pale butterfly
in morning's damp heat
flapping lazy spirals through
the open kitchen window

daVinci might have built this
with feathery bits of tissue
engineered a pair of sticks
plaything for an angel

The Twelve Colours of Darkness

And, in the isolation of the sky,
At evening, casual flocks of pigeons make
Ambiguous undulations as they sink,
Downward to darkness, on extended wings.

from *"Sunday Morning"*
Wallace Stevens

Life of the Finch: Interior Shadows

the small birds are worrying

about cats that can fly
attacking them in trees
stealing nests as decorations
wearing straw and feathers
in amongst their fur and claws
like grinning ancient generals
smiling drunk at all the wet

no wonder the birds are screaming
banshees from some tired star
clutching fronds of cedar
rattled bones in wind

Shadow in Sunlight

such sunny days and Len lies dying in a bed
much too stiff and white with crispened sheets
while here I sit folded in a soggy red robe
softness of its terrycloth holds me to my chair
ready to ground any shimmering bolts of hope
capture reassurance that might rain down from the sky

catching at the dusty moths
this summer afternoon
patches of their rustled wings
tremble in my hand

like an owl caught out in daylight
prowling where it shouldn't be
shadow of an airplane
passes cross my body
shiver of uncertainty
shudders down the length of me

Once Upon a Time the Little Match Girl

my mother told us fairy tales
hopeless homemade stories
made me always love the ones
with depressing endings
Wild Swans
Broken Sparrow
always made me cry
best of all the saddest
Little Match Girl

she made me love the girls in them
their shabby broken ways
staunchest resignation
gritting through the toughest times
very nearly getting by
or better yet dying
holey mittens lying in a snowbank

but better even when she told
stories that were true
sisters nearly eight and just-eleven
straggling home that evening
through pale December light
dragging home a sled that held
chunks of coal they'd found beside

rails behind the factory that built tractors
blowing on their fingertips
measuring every corner
trading turns at tugging the rope
pulling the load back home

and when the welfare gave out clothes
she'd been so delighted
spun a little dance around the kitchen near the stove
wore the outfit proudly till
she went to school again
saw that other girl across
the rows of wooden desks
wearing the identical
dress of straight maroon
saw its plainness lack of frill
no longer thought it pretty
match girls holding pockets full of secrets

Canning Peaches

I never understood
why they called it canning fruits
when everyone always used jars

my sister and I scrounge around
in among the spiders
rifle through the shelves behind the furnace
gather all those glassy shapes
careful not to crack them
rinse them in the tubs beside
the washer with its wringer
silent with its threat of mangled hands
stack them in a basket
then cart them up the stairs
each of us with fingers through
the creaky wicker handles

the sink up in the kitchen
would be filling with the peels
fuzzy strips of brown and orange
curling from our mother's knife
bruising peaches in a pile
looking soft as babies' heads
fontanelle the spot you couldn't touch

standing by my newest sister
I watch bubbles from her lip
while she lies asleep
her ribboned basket on the floor
I pat the small indention
breathy hole atop her head
wanting more than anything
push my thumb and see
think about those peaches
coasting dark behind the glass
each one with its floating pit
some hopeless brown brain

hear my mother's voice sing low
hush my little angel
picture babies sleeping there
sideways in a jar

Trains in the Night

trains in the night always come from such a distance
gather a shape in front of them as they near

like long thin clouds bundled together pushing the wind
bringing rains to beat so hard and sharp against the land

their thunder lingers on grumbling low into the black
rumbling long and far into the darkness

We are as Summer Heat

we are as summer heat
temporary on this world
shimmering
we appear
and disappear

as the earth calls down forks of lightning deep unto itself
sharp in the damp heat of August-ripened fields
so you and I yield our bodies each to each
singeing magnets power surge
pressing hard like flattened knives
soldered fast together in some steel furnaced heat

I have seen a Tesla coil
shoot blue wind cross the room
its crackled slash of energy bounce high into the air
balance of another kind
caught-up forces in the sky
constantly undone again
redone and then repeated

memory of jagged light
fades off in the distance

Siamese Twin II

they move their small hands
pat their heads
a state of alarm

finding only air
where each other
used to be

so are we
seeking wholeness
in the night we make together

an apple sliced in half
pressed back close
entire again

for a slippery fleeting moment
we succeed
not even a seam

AFTER VISITING A FRIEND'S PARROT, JUNGLE NIGHTMARES PERSIST

after bombs and beatings
and cars that explode in the night
reincarnation is yet another terror
deterrent to suicide

i.
so no other man in the village would want me
find his own use for the pleasures I might bring
you took my fingers
naming each one
careful as you sliced it away
Esmeraude, Jonquille, Sativa
till I fainted
woke with ragged fists
lamenting the memory of touch

ii.
after the moon had changed again
your mother unwrapped the cloths
let me grieve the flattened clubs
thick and heavy on my arms

but you kept me nearby
through the cold of that long winter
fastened always to the bed
a chain of golden silk

iii.
you who were a king then
have now become a bird
live in a cage lined with mirrors and bells
its shape a sombre dome near a window

talons of your bony feet
extend from deep within
sheaths of withered grey
like wrinkled homely foreskin

shining claws like fingers curl
around your wooden perch
clipped tips of your futile wings
useless in even a breeze

iv.
still we share a tango
bob a rhythm eye to eye

tune plucked from a violin
weeps wildly on the radio
drives your maddened stepping
crazy dance beside the firelit wall
flickered shapes the fever of fear
mingled with shadows from lifetimes ago

both of us hold memories
your body locked in mine
still can taste the bitter pain of joy

v.
balanced
in a silvered cage
the parrot king
atones

POISON IN THE BLOODSTREAM

squeezing drops from my bladder
as if it were a lemon
measly and acidic
slow burn in the night
still getting rid of you
poison in the bloodstream

burn this
when you finish it
measure the smoke
for venom

Rev. Peacock and the Church of the Ten Thousand Bats

he has convinced them of his brilliance
as he skulks within his coat
twirls those thousand hidden eyes
looking ever inward

holding closed his feathered ruff
some secret hand of cards
he rustles frills of dust across the wide cavern floor
scratches tracks of sand each time he passes

glints of opalescence
squint beneath his cloak
his tail like sullen roses
drags a trail across the dirt

his private horde of furried bats
clings stalwart upside down
lined in rows so tight they knit
rough carpets for the ceiling

accustomed to the pitch of dark their tiny eyes survey
his endless pacing forth and back
the grainy wake he leaves behind
alert to widen and fly at only the hint of his command

how worshipfully they wait for his urge to coalesce
rustle soft among themselves muttering expectant
hope the blessed plumes will soon
take heed of them and open
sanctify the quiet inner glory of their night

MISTAKEN IDENTITY: A POEM TO MY FATHER

so was it all just some big mistake
that summer night slinking careful
up the narrow stairs
past the landlady and her dog
the two of you tangling quiet
in the knot of sweated sheets
trying to ride so silent
lie thin behind the walls

was it something you had to prove
to your buddies back at the bar
that the young one   such a looker
could go for you   kind of an old guy
fresh home from the war
full of stories and too much booze
how they leaned their chins on their elbows
watched you lead her through tavern doors
to the cool of summer nightfall
light as a sundress on your arm

so who might have ever expected
that the night would turn into a baby
still a reason back then for a wedding
all those promises of forever

going through the motions
doing all you were expected
was there any other choice
was there one you could have lived with

and then the years went flapping past
like curtains slapping wind
one by one across your face full of accusations
me only the first in line   all those straight-haired girls
tall and lanky-awkward string   endless disappointments
hanging out to dry across a lifetime

tell me now about those times
regrets at all those daughters
not a son among the batch
not a single one
not a son to somehow maybe
justify it
all

By the Light within the Body

"The stars were huge, like daisies through the windowpanes."
— May Sarton

in that place there were miners
toiling underneath the sea
working with such steadiness
below the quiet ice

terrible frigid radiance
held us in its grasp
trapped but swimming faithfully
Chagall legs paddle silent

rising to extol the light
near but never there
lungs like popping fireworks
taunting not atoning

by the light within the body
we work our way toward morning

Seasons of the Blind

*Icarus understood zero
as he caught the smell
of burning feathers
and fell into the sea*

from *"Poem About Nothing"*
Lorna Crozier

Free Flight

driving fast toward Fraser Bridge
going to my sister's house
she of nervous breakdown fame
previous and current

as always I must marvel at this tenuous creation
hanging here in space between the city and the sky
grey lanes pointing both ways
with no one goin' nowhere
blanketed in thick morning fog

especially not me
engine seized here on the Honda
much more rust than paint on this ol' babe

one of my kids in the back
is puking up his breakfast
this makes the other one cry
the noise he makes very nearly drowns out the siren
needling its way through the tangle of cars
stuck out here behind us this otherwise lovely day

and somehow wouldn't ya know it
the cop weasels through
thick stub of a ticket book attached to his hand

pulls up right behind me daring me to move
from where I've made my unplanned stop
in the passing lane

me
I just enjoy the view
this cat's cradle of wires
admire how it's all that holds us up above the river
imagine myself climbing
Spider Woman in the riggings
swinging out on pendulums of web
winging out and letting go downward to the water

laughing
laughing loud
crazy laughing
all
the
way
down

In Among the Rednecks, Part One

racing up the Sunshine Coast
looking for a cheap motel
just a lazy place
to lay our bones
stand under a shower

dusk is nearly ended here
but so then is the highway
quarter tank of gas
and half a pack of smokes
sweat is maybe all
that keeps us going

three raised-up pick-up trucks
lunge from someone's driveway
line themselves a convoy
in the track of our rearview
two sagging Pontiacs slow us down in front

just beyond the clear-cut
between curves along the road
we start to get the picture
cram our baseball hats down low
try to think like locals   fit the scenery

pass so close between the row
of cedars and salal
I expect a branch will scrape the car

the road a narrow room that twists
dust combined with steam
rising from the mist of rain
first we've had all summer

balanced on that yellow line
tourist paranoia

In Among the Rednecks, Part Two

so we all are really rednecks
at heart
so deep inside
secretly
we love that country music

we know all the words
to *Heartbreak Hotel*
can harmonize a medley
Williams   Patsy Cline
but won't yet go and do
no karaoke
at the bar

still we yodel
in the shower
at the height of summer moon
warble to the din
of heated waters
sing beneath its soft massage
pink skin rising

IN THE BATH, WITH A COMPANION

I reach to pull the plug
drain this lazy Saturday bath
there is a spider
suspended
sharing water with me

filament legs and comma body
some astronaut lost in space
dragging still the knotted ropes
his almost-finished web
unfurls itself behind him
silken dressing gown untied
floating open   languishing undone

it billows a cloud around him
leaky parachute   soft and hopeless
in an atmosphere that hasn't any wind

      the other day the shuttle crew
      testing jet packs wandered out
      entering that silent hole
      empty long forgetfulness
      cast themselves unbound into
      the black night of space

moving in slow motion like underwater divers
their steps are puffs of breathy tai-chi

stars they say don't twinkle there
the moon doesn't rise
water doesn't flow in a circle counter-clockwise

but this murky water moves in swirls
between my knees
while the spider spins off
to his own eternity

Sizing Up the Omens

(Hornby Island, January 1)

we walk along the beachhead
deserted in the winter damp
ghosts of last year's drummers
all that linger from July

today   only waves
play their rhythms to the air
rolling massive rocks   giant marbles round the shallows
back across the line defining ocean land and ocean

underneath the cliff base   we step a wary dance
balance over crevices that seethe a seaweed foam
nearly fall across a corpse
broken deer sprawled out on stone

legs splayed   staring eye
hopeless   to the sky
its gaze as round as barnacles etched on rock beside it
still full of surprise at having fallen this far
one leg pokes its way up from
the thickened coat so furred
a question mark lying there still puzzling

even the deer
are raining down the cliff face
bodies tumbling quiet through thick of morning air
boding not much promise for this foggy new year

Post-op

you show me your bandage
how it reaches way beneath your arm
around to almost your back

the line of you so smooth now
we should call this part   something else
no longer any hint of breast to fondle or to hold

as if we are little girls again
flat chests running bare
hot in the bold face of summer
nipples tiny pebbles on the surface of our shining skin
breast no longer the word
for what you wear there

DOMESTIC HUSBANDRY

the women had all spent
too much time behind water
standing by kitchen sinks
moving dishes around

seeing the faces that shimmered in foam
after nearly all of the bubbles had gone
swirls of floating olive oil displaying private casts
voices carrying accents heavy as stones

earthly concerns nothing
that wouldn't be solved eventually
with the addition of steam
sufficient heat   or soapings

THE CHICKEN BUILDS AN EMPIRE IN AN OCEAN OF DUST

the hen has decided to abandon the house
crowded with feathered brethren
squawking all those senseless conversations

she has left behind her wild-haired nest
forsaken the pile of broken tan
shells littered on the ground so
many babies dead or stolen

scratches instead at
a rock in the yard
every day so patient

draws a line across the stone
carefully places one long toe
fitting her claw precisely in
the wedge of its craven notch

the same imagined groove
she visits it every day
over and over
marking a sign
reminding herself
she's been here

DINNER NOTES TO MY HUSBAND
ABOUT MY BIRTHDAY CALL

again this morning when she phoned
my mother was bewildered
this time thought that you'd been born in Thailand

confusing some friend's holiday with
where we might have met
all those years between us disappeared to her

impressive the creation of imaginings she shared
surprised to hear your mother can
speak English   drive a car

I conjure her inventing you growing up in Asia
wading slow in shallow ponds
pulling hard to haul the catch
slapping fish caught up so tight within the strings and mesh
nets you wove at nighttime with
your father under stars

she prefers this movie scene   intoxicating views
selects a dream in harmony with years of blue denial
doesn't want to hear about the heat of a tobacco farm
off the highway somewhere in Ontario

too mundane to think about you
in between the rows
sweating in the sunlight of a muggy afternoon
snakes amid the dust for decoration
bending toward the flattened earth
pulling off the golden leaves
crowned around the base of all
those blonde-haired furry stems
filling up a another box ready for the kiln-house bake
racing with your brothers to the end of another row

⁓

I guess my mother pictures us
as wildly-plumed exotic birds
flying in from warmer climes
like long-lost foreign cousins
that she lives in dreams about
a ballroom marble-cool
swirling circles round and round
a blurry satin gown
wants to be some Anna with
her King of Siam

ENGINEER OF PAIN

*"If the lever and fulcrum are capable of moving the world, surely it
must be the humble flywheel that actually keeps it all in motion. It
contains the secrets of the universe within its quiet simplicity..."*
— *Unknown*

I.
turning in rusty concentrics
circles each smaller
within the other's arc

tightening the grip
we hold on one other
afraid to let go

of spinning off
the face of the map
far into the space of forgotten

II.
the van painted here and there
patches of bygone care
embroidered on a field of open rust

but then finally
its wheels would turn
only to the right

planning the trip
to the junkyard that night
took all of us nearly till dawn

arrows on the open map
spiralling a path
across the blank face of the city

crashing from the acid
in corners of the house
crumpled bundles lying paired

or quiet and alone
everyone slept badly
in tangled fuzzy dreams

sparks of light that buzzed in trails
like sloppy signatures
lingering and airborne   barely out of reach

III.
a man plays out bad justice from the far end of a table
its surface is a blurry map of branded coffee rings
faded to a scrawl of lapping circles

        furry-looking caterpillar
        trails from burning cigarettes
        long ago forgotten leave criss-crossed paths

markers blazing always
in the heart
of the wood

he has made an artform
snipping parts off living things
bits of skin and hangnails torn

quick between the teeth
better skilled than tweezer's edge
sharpened fingers work the night

pinch the hairy filament
bent sharply at the knee
from dumb and unsuspecting daddy longlegs

he has practised this craft
understands precisely
just how many legs it takes

to keep the spider upright
balanced
if still teetering

tiny parasol in its jaws
prancing on the tightrope
linking gravity and death

he appreciates which wing parts
he can pincer-grip away
so the wasp will buzz a flight

around the room
dazzling
a kite on invisible strings

he can formulate the method
keep the fly in careful spin
scribbling tired circles   round and bluey-black

shining in its fading   iridescence
how to keep it hovering there barely just above
the dirty scarred surface of this mean battleground

where no rules
are the only law
and power is in the hands of the large

stumps of roaches
bleeding brown
into a dusty ashtray

what a sight
for the dying
to remember

the path of its ellipse
reaches arms around the room
to the right

to the right
ending always to the right
in its numbed half-perception

the insect still is thinking
it's on a straight line
to escape

OLD WIVES' TALE

if a fishbone
should lodge itself
sideways in the throat
do not let its hardness
deceive you

find three yellow plums
just gone
past their perfection
eat them very slowly
keep their juices
in your mouth

avoid excessive chewing
let them glide down while they hold
semblance of the flesh still thick upon them
swallow
let the pits slide
sweetly cleansing as they move

by morning
dig a hole
with your fingers
in the earth
shit there
close it carefully

with tea leaves
steamed all night

go away for many years
on a boat with coloured sails
wander back when you are old
glory in the garden
trees leaning heavy
golden plums

Acres of Sunlight

Like the back of my hand, *we say*
for the place we come to call home,
the claim we can only make
through the hands, planting food and children . . .

Who am I to say what distances he should believe in . . .

from *"Distance from Harrowsmith to Tamworth"*
Bronwen Wallace

ALBERTA VISITOR

houses here   so far from anything
make me want to knock on doors
ask   how did I/you
ever get here

I am used to
small rocks
worn smooth
by water and time

my eyes keep straining
looking for   the ocean
on this landscape
with too many   horizons

PARANOID

in the jungle we carry our fears
like eggs in a paper bag
minor jostling's all it takes to shatter their fragile shells
spill them down the front of our shirts for anyone to see
goods no longer contained within
the safety of themselves

I step my way on tiptoe through
this world of writhing vines
tree trunks green with sinews that lurk
weird in contortionary poses

see a snake in every root
winding its curled way over the path
find the print of reptile scales
in even the tread from a mountain bike
gone this way before us
spinning past in all this mud

can't help but imagine
the lair of some fabulous python
overgrown and brown with spots
fatter than any branch

remind myself that he is bound
by gravity more than by cunning
nonetheless I worry
try to walk on air

PEGGI MAKES A HOUSECALL

(Caye Caulker, Belize)

although we're on holiday
middle of the night
a woman comes pounding at our door
begs us   nearly strangers
to please let her in
hush the light and bar the lock
quick before he finds her

only the tip of her burning cigarette
bleeds its orange glow into the room
illuminates the line of her chin as she speaks
all you and I can do is listen to what she says
hear the broken words as they twist
from the side of her mouth

     how he held her by the neck
     cradled her head against the step
     bashed it there again   and again
     told her to be quiet
     not to wake up any neighbours
     try to show some class   for a change

this morning over coffee
her hand is a shaking bird
poking its way from inside the sleeve of

the shirt that's way too big on her
the one she borrowed nearly dawn
the one she finally slept in

the home-made tattoo rides a line on her wrist
its purpled blue the same tone as
the bruises now kissing her jaw

she talks about her children
close in months but so far apart
their fights such steady warfare
who could know that they are brothers
how the nine-year-old sometimes scares her
has already become a stranger
tells us this isn't the only time
this man of hers has hurt her
and I can see it in her swollen eye
she will sleep with him tonight

Backgammon for Breakfast

La Manzanilla, Mexico

mockingbirds and flycatchers engage in conversation
chasing insects back and forth in time
and all the while the worn out backhoe squeaks and
    creaks its way
ka-chung-ging cross the landscape scraping soil
machine gears groaning back and forth grade away
    the mountaintop
flatten it for view lots fancy houses for us *gringos*
slicing so relentlessly
against the warmth of earth
breaking down the tallest trees all those years in growing
raking roots like so much clutter tossing them aside
forgotten beer tins plastic bags and empty paper cups
roadways shaping zigzagged up the hillside

in between time all those animals
confused as displaced persons
caught out in the aftermath of sudden summer storm
wander in a dazzle of hardening bewilderment
unnamed birds disoriented fly in puzzled circles
seek out nests with babies who were hungry just
    this morning
even wayward turkey buzzards waft upon the breezes
aimless as if lost at sea their senses gone awry
so much death their beaks are full and streaked

with drying blood
endlessly they carry on unceasing in their flights
plunder dismal carrion the unforgiving feast
cargo for the cleansing of their gizzards

no wonder the gliding snake crawled down
sneaky just last week
brazen jungle visitor that uninvited guest
let himself in keyless through the iron-grated window
Marco's room while everyone *siesta'd*
drew his body up into the golden songbirds' cage
ate his fill with two of them
in plain view of the other pair
alarming them for days beyond the hope of any song
then found himself shut in as well
belly scales humped out too far
to fit back through the bony bars retreat to slinky freedom

and here we sit together fat in prisons all our own
credit worries mortgaged lives children run away
peppering our calendars with compensating schemes
counting up invented scams sunlit days of lotto dreams
determining elusive winning numbers
yet all the time with nervous eyes we're glancing at the bluff
even as we shake a batch of sticky *margaritas*
roll the dice for one more game line up the clacking pieces
suck back cold *cervezas* topped with thinly sliced *limones*
gathered in this morning's round of lazy windfall harvest

waiting for that piled up mound of muddled earth
    the world
to topple down and settle this match
    once and for all

SEX IN THE TROPICS

I.

the couple from Miami
taught us all a lesson
it seems too many flea bites
can strain a new relationship
her perfect white ass
not so perfect anymore
a constellation
reddened bites
cools his big dipper

the two of them fly out of here
depart on separate planes
one behind the other
rising straight up and mad
hard into the fiery light of dawn
they leave a swirl of rising dust
the scream of engines thrusting
something for the locals
near the airstrip to remember

II.

construction boys from Canada
have gone uptown and scored big time
laughing girls from Germany
a blonde and a brunette
Christmas treats should last for the duration

we could hear the four of them
fucking loud and long last night

everyone seems more relaxed
can feel the tension ease
as after rain the steam can finally rise

all of us drink less now
in the morning

III.
Sal is bragging loudly
two *Juanitas* already today
after coffees and a spliff he sits dreamy

savouring the flavours
on his fingers Susanne and Maria
admiring their tastes as if they are beautiful rings

he sits beneath the lazy fan
in his father's restaurant
slowly eats a plate of rice and beans

squints across the chairs in the room
his eyes the only thing moving fast
scanning the horizon for dessert

ODE TO PERSEVERANCE

three long days it floated in the white bowl of the toilet
much too full of angst and dark black beans to go away
a testament to stubbornness and cheap *Latino* plumbing
disdaining every passerby a multitude of flushings

glaring up defiant   ready to growl at any who look
gaze upon its brownness cast their pee upon its form
an insult to all pretence of mannerly refinement
brazen challenge trapped there coiled and snarling

steadfastly giving the finger   fat and long

Bus Station

(Limon, Costa Rica)

diesel fumes so thick here
the air is one long breath of tar
how many days to clear the taste
from my lungs my skin

everyone quietly munches for salt
faces all hid by potato chip sacks
bags to our faces like oxygen masks
we could be riding some spiralling plane

but here we all wait for the bus to Cahuita
other points south or off to the west
sit hunkered over in kind of a line
curled so tight up against the curb

CRAB DANCE

transparent land crab no bigger than my fist
honky-tonks his way
      keying sideways down the beach
plays his sandy piano just for me

stops to look me over rolls his eyes in every direction
wants to find some jazzy chick
      auditioning tonight
but doesn't even listen to my song

closes his piano starts another soft shoe dance
makes his sorry way in drunken bursts across the sand
      dropping in a hole to mend
his lopsided heart

ACRES OF SUNLIGHT ON A SONNET
EVERLASTING: FOR CAMELLIA

Cahuita, Costa Rica

Vanessa is teaching her daughter
      tropical baby
the language of birds
trilling cockles, whistles, *burrahs*
         into the folds of her tiny brown ear

while canary twirrs a steady stream melodic conversation
to the gawking ocean parrot
quirrah-quawking on his perch
high up in the palm tree near the window

slowly
as the months grow
even parrots learn to sing

The Question of Dawn

When the last day comes
a ploughman in Europe will look over his shoulder
and see the hard furrows of earth
finally behind him...

It will be morning
for the first time, and the long night
will be seen for what it is,
a black flag trembling in the sunlight.

from *"The Last Day"*
Kevin Hart

The Body Finds Its Own Ways to Speak for Us All: Song for the One-Legged Man

the two of us sat riding in the cool air of the white car
eyes steady on the long road pointing the way toward home
while she told me of the pain he rode so strenuous he'd sweat

water that would pour its way from his paling body
first in dots that rose across his ever-greyer skin
then spurt in growing streams to glide gathering unbidden
in quiet tired puddles on the sheets underneath him

but after such a short time that succour was withheld
his steadily thinning body blocking even that small ease
as if everything inside of him had dried in tight refusal
denying him all comfort the tiniest reliefs

so then she'd sat and told him every good thing she remembered
whispered all the secrets she could think of in his ear
and when she finally knew that there was nothing left to tell
he'd loosened his thick fingers from her hand

> *lesser than the clasp we knew*
> *arm-wrestling his way*
> *through life as if it were some*
> *swirling carnival ride*

its insane inane calamities
swinging you upside down
crazy air catching hard
banging your fist back down

forever letting go his grip on her and on this life
finally exhaling   giving in to the peace of it all
finding himself that place he had dreamed
so long and white and clean
heading out and into it   clear with measured strides

WINTERSCAPE

the landscape is frozen
so hard and so white
it hurts my eyes to look
outside this window

the shadow of an angel
lies fallen on the snow
in the spot where I lay yesterday
and dumbly moved my limbs

COUNTRY WESTERN POEM

you never
ran me over
with the car
    baby
you never
shot me once
with a gun
    hon
and you never
did give me
a child
    baby
but darlin
we sure had some fun

yes you always knew well how to make me feel small
you always could turn me from glad into sad
you always would tell me how crazy I was
and darlin you sure could get mad

now sometimes I think of my life spent with you
sometimes I wonder just how it could be
sometimes I dream of those days long gone by
and think we were just like TV

no you never
ran me over
with the car
    (didja) baby
you never
did shoot me
with a gun
        honeybun
and you never
made me
crazy (though ya tried)
        sweetheart
but darlin
we sure had some fun

Brown Dog

out here on the farm now
three summers in a row

still shy
when the man comes too near
lifts his hand

for anything

PASTORAL

ducks on the pond tow their babies in a row
pull them behind on a line only they can see
even so the ducklings seem nervous   look around
afraid that they might lose the trail
invisible on water

and yea as I walk through the bursting springtime field
the sheep all seem to yell at my approach
MAAAD or BAD   depending on their moods
whatever paranoias they hide behind their masks
worried I might want to steal the tenderest of shoots
pinch the newest tips from every flower
beat them to the tasty bits before they make their way
stumble their rumbling mouths across the meadow

I pick my way among the prickling thistles freshened nettles
tiptoe to miss squishing any fat black shiny slugs
draped lazily on bending stems of hapless sweet weeds

a plethora of mint leaf grows relentless in this field
yet the grinding sheep ignore the allure of its temptation
resist the invitation of its deeply scented leaves
step around it carefully   black shoes a *rond-de-loo*

do they give it such wide berth because
they know what it is served with
is the reason they so bleat at me
despite my careful tread
they can tell I am an eater
of mint and roasted lamb

bless us o lord and these thy friends
whom we are about to receive

Walking on the Day Before the First Day of Spring

branches of some fruiting tree
or maybe just magnolia
reach up to this first blue sky
it seems in so many months

buds gleam like swollen heads
of freshly sucked dicks
glistening and full
of so much promise

PROMISES,, PROMISES

I will ride my red motorcycle
into your heart
crash land my feelings
all over your doorstep
fling scented pink petals
across your front lawn
kiss you like pancakes
for breakfast

GROUPIE

me
I just wanna marry
the Zamboni driver
he looks all reliable
a steady kind of guy

it really turns me on
the way he makes those zooming sweeps
perfect down the whole length of the ice
how he speeds it up so fast
pushing when he swings so tight
hard into the turn inside the corner

love his handsome face
riding high on that machine
wonder will I love him still
after
the game

Making Out with the Editor

he runs his critical eye
down the length of her
page
pulling small mistakes
from the body
of text
like teasing broken threads
from a button half-loose
dawdling his hands
over too many
howevers
encountering a swollen
nevertheless

his strong fingers
touch the space
in each tight
semicolon

breathless
she pants
into the comma
of his ear
shut your eyes
dammit all
kiss me

ADAM AND EVE AND FUCK ME
(for RK)

If God ever really existed
and so did Paradise
you have to wonder what it was
that started all the fuss

I bet it wasn't Eve or Adam
eating some old apple
that got them both kicked out of
that Bible story Eden

I think it was asparagus
cheeky tips all poking green
firm as horny penises shoving hard through earth
something God was keeping for Himself

trouble was the stinking stream
of next day's morning pee
wafted out the secret of their early springtime feast
odour like a green guilt rising upward with its steam

they don't need any bushes now
they do it loud outside
not caring whether angels gods or serpents want to watch
they drape themselves all sexy   done up in twining vines

Secret Gardener: The Biologist

I grow nasturtiums
their wrinkled seeds like tiny scrotum
hard   make you want to hold them   gentle
between your teeth

and sometimes geraniums
their dusty metal smell
spermy kind of perfume
on my fingers

Yet Another Season by Your Side

already
these mornings
grey hairs shine
from in your beard

while you sleep
I rise quiet
go outside
into the angled light

pick a bowl of berries
careful
from their nests
all the while
tangled thorns
are grabbing at my hair

blackberries
so fat and sweet
something I can grow for you
one thing
I can still bring
feed you every summer

HEIDI GRECO is an editor and writer who has lived in the Vancouver area since 1970. Her book reviews have appeared in newspapers and magazines across the country, including the *Vancouver Sun, subTerrain* and *Paragraph*. Her poems have been published in numerous magazines, as well as having been included in anthologies in both Canada and the U.S.

Ms. Greco's work comprised one third of the poetry triptych *Siren Tattoo* (Anvil Press).